Published by Scholastic Inc.
90 Old Sherman Turnpike, Danbury, Connecticut 06816.

For information regarding permission, write to:
Disney Licensed Publishing
114 Fifth Avenue, New York, New York 10011.

ISBN 0-7172-8492-1

Designed and produced by Bill SMITH STUDIO.

Printed in the U.S.A.
First printing, September 2002

The Mixed-up Morning

A Story About
Taking Turns

by **Jacqueline A. Ball**
illustrated by **Caveman Productions**

SCHOLASTIC INC.

New York Toronto London Auckland Sydney
Mexico City New Delhi Hong Kong Buenos Aires

Outside the cottage of the Seven Dwarfs, the morning sun was rising.

In the kitchen, Snow White stirred a big pot over the fire. "Mmm," she said, taking a sniff. "The porridge is ready. I'll toast the bread, and then the Dwarfs' breakfast will be done."

Quickly Snow White sliced some bread.
"Cheep! Cheep!" the birds sang.
"What did you say?" she laughed. "Oh, you want breakfast, too. Well, line up!"

The princess scooped up a handful of bread crumbs. One by one, the birds hopped over and ate them out of her hand.

When the birds had finished, Snow White ran to the stairs. "Sleepy! Grumpy! Doc! Bashful! Dopey! Sneezy! Happy!" she called. "Breakfast is ready!"

$\mathcal{T}$he Dwarfs tumbled from their beds.

"Mmm," sighed Happy. "Smell that toast! How wonderful!"

"Maybe the princess has made porridge, too," said Sneezy.

"Just for us?" asked Bashful, turning red.

"Well, I'm hungrier than anyone," Grumpy grunted. "So I'm going to wash first."

"No," said Doc. "I want to fo gurst—I mean, go first!"

Grumpy and Doc tugged at the wash bucket, each one trying to be first.

*S*PLASH! The big bucket of water splashed all over Dopey.

"Oops! Sorry, Dopey!" Doc said, apologizing.

"I told you I should have gone first!" Grumpy muttered.

"*I* need the comb," Happy announced.

"No, I do," Sneezy said.

Happy and Sneezy grabbed the same comb and tried to comb their beards.

*H*appy and Sneezy looked in the mirror.

Their beards were all tangled and knotted together.

"Oh, no!" Sneezy exclaimed.

"Now what will we do?" cried Happy.

"Ahhhh—

As the two Dwarfs tried to untangle their
beards, Sneezy let loose a gigantic sneeze.

hoooo!!"

*T*he sneeze separated Sneezy's and Happy's beards, sending the Dwarfs flying.

The Dwarfs hurried to finish getting ready.

"You're in my way!" Grumpy snapped
at Sleepy.

"That's—*yawn!*—*my* hat!" Sleepy told Bashful.

"Uh, that's my jacket," Bashful said to Happy.

"*W*hat a mix-up!" sighed Happy.

A few moments later, Snow White called to the Dwarfs. "Please, hurry! Your breakfast is getting cold!"

The Dwarfs raced down the stairs, each trying to be first. They tumbled and bounced all the way down, landing in a heap.

"Whose foot is on my head?" Sleepy asked sleepily.

"You're mitting on see!" Doc mumbled. "I mean you're sitting on me!"

"What a muddle!" groaned Sneezy.

The Dwarfs scrambled into their seats.

Sneezy and Happy both grabbed for the milk at the same time. *SPLASH!*

Grumpy and Doc both tried to spoon porridge into their bowls. *SPLAT!*

Dopey and Sleepy both tugged at the same piece of toast. *CRUNCH!*

"Miss is a thess—I mean, this is a mess!" cried Doc. All the other Dwarfs became quiet.

"It certainly is," Snow White agreed. "See what happens when you don't take turns? Now, please, clean it up."

$\mathcal{A}$fter the Dwarfs had cleaned up the table, Snow White handed each of them a slice of bread with jam. "Don't worry," she said. "There's enough for everyone."

Once they had finished eating, the princess said, "Now run and get your things."

Snow White went to the kitchen. She had made a picnic lunch for the Dwarfs to take with them. She took the basket, walked outside, and waited while the Dwarfs were rushing about inside.

*D*oc took his lantern.

Grumpy hoisted his pickaxe.

Sleepy got his shovel.

*H*appy picked up his hammer.

Dopey took his bucket.

Sneezy got his rope.

Bashful grabbed his work gloves.

All the Dwarfs got to the front door at the same time.

"*M*e first!" grumbled Grumpy, shoving the others. "No, me first!" said Happy.

Snow White watched as each Dwarf struggled to get through first. Her friends had certainly had a mixed-up, muddled, messy morning.

What would a princess do?

" My, my my! Everyone can't fit through the door at once," Snow White told them.

The Dwarfs went back inside and sat down.

"Look what happened this morning when you all tried to do everything at the same time," Snow White said. "Now, please, try it again—one at a time."

"*G*reat idea!" shouted Grumpy.
"One at a time. But I'll go first!"

"Oh, no, you don't!" said Sneezy.
"*I'll* go first!"

"No, me!" cried Happy.

"Oh, dear!" Snow White said, shaking her head. "Everyone can't be first at the same time. You'll have to take turns being first."

"*H*mm," Grumpy mumbled, stroking his beard. "How do we do that?"

"Well," Snow White began, "there are seven days in a week, right?"

"Well, yes," said Doc.

"And there are seven of you, right?"

Dopey started to count, became confused, and started again.

"That's right," Happy added.

"So every week, each of you will have his own special day to be first!" the princess explained. "I can even make a list to help you remember."

The Seven Dwarfs agreed that this was a very good idea.

"Here, Bashful," Snow White said, handing him the basket. "Today is your day to be first."

Bashful blushed. "Thanks, Princess," he said shyly as he took the basket.

One by one, the Dwarfs walked outside.

Snow White waved good-bye
as they marched to work, singing:

Just take . . . your turn.

And you will surely learn

That one by one

Is much more fun.

Just take . . . your turn!

The End